HERRERASAURUS

DSUNGARIPTERUS

STYGIMOLOCH

CENTROSAURUS

MONOLOPHOSAURUS

SEGNOSAURUS

IGUANODON

SILVISAURUS

DIPLODOCUS

CERATOSAURUS

For dino-mite editor Bonnie Verburg,
who has always loved these books! ~ J. Y.

To Bonnie Verburg, for making great books,
and to Kathy Westray, for making them beautiful. ~ M. T.

First published in hardback by The Blue Sky Press, an Imprint of Scholastic Inc., USA, in 2007
First published in paperback in Great Britain by HarperCollins Children's Books in 2007

1 3 5 7 9 10 8 6 4 2

ISBN-13: 978-0-00-725817-8
ISBN-10: 0-00-725817-8

HarperCollins Children's Books is a division of HarperCollins Publishers Ltd.

Text copyright © Jane Yolen 2007
Illustrations copyright © Mark Teague 2007

JANE YOLEN
How Do Dinosaurs
Go to School?

Illustrated by

MARK TEAGUE

HarperCollins *Children's Books*

How does a dinosaur
go to school?
Does he walk?
Does he ride in
a busy car pool?

CENTROSAURUS

Does he drag his long tail?
Is he late for the bus?
Does he stomp all four feet?
Does he make a big fuss?

When he gets to the school

Does he play fight and punch?

Does he make a quick grab

for a classmate's packed lunch?

Does he race up the stairs
right ahead of the bell?

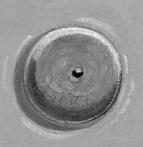

STYGIMOLOCH

Does he interrupt class
with his own show-and-tell?

DOES A
DINOSAUR
YELL?

And when in the classroom,
plonked down in his chair,
does a dinosaur fidget,
his tail in the air?

Does he growl
during lessons,
or roar out of turn?

Does he make it too hard
for the others to learn?

Does he stir up
the classroom
by making
a noise?

Does he tease all the girls?

Does he pick on the boys?

No...

A dinosaur carefully
raises his hand.

He helps out his classmates
with projects

they've planned.

At break time he plays
with a number of friends
and growls at the bullies
till bullying ends.

He tidies his desk,
then he leaps
out the door.

Good work.

Good work, little dinosaur.